Dear Love

Grant Gosch

central
avenue
2025

Content Warning:

This book contains explicit scenes of a sexual nature
and is intended for mature audiences only.

Published by Central Avenue Poetry, an imprint of Central Avenue Marketing Ltd.
www.centralavenuepublishing.com

DEAR LOVE

Trade Paper: 978-1-77168-392-0
Ebook: 978-1-77168-393-7

Published in Canada
Printed in United States of America

1. POETRY / Subjects & Themes - Love   2. Poetry / American

1 3 5 7 9 10 8 6 4 2

This book is dedicated to the vulnerable souls
who shared their love with me. Thank you for
the gift of an open heart.

XO

I am a romantic. I always have been. It took me some time to embrace this part of my being, but now I hold it with pride. I'm glad to be a romantic.

Once claimed, I wanted to share my romantic heart. Sometimes, sharing is a deeper form of claiming, so I posted an all-call on Instagram asking my audience to share love letter requests with me. I asked them to share the context and the spice level of the letter they wanted.

I received requests from around the world. And, I'll tell you what, people love spice.

This book is an attempt to honor the requests I received. Some letters are erotic, some are playful, and some show the human interpretation of love between animals. All of the letters are heartfelt and written from my romantic soul to yours. I hope this book inspires you to say, "Yes! I am a romantic. And I'm proud of it."

XO

Unite

Dear Love,

I don't know what I noticed first. I keep trying to place it. Just when I think it was your denim shorts I stop myself and think, no, it was the smell of sunscreen.

I don't know.

I do know that noticing you was a full-body experience. You, so brown and smooth and smelling of SPF 30 at least.

You walked by, and I was done for.

The first pursuit of my life.

I stood before being conscious of standing. I swayed like a drunk as I pushed through the door that opened onto the galley. I found you by the window. The wind danced your hair back and over your shoulder. You turned and looked at me.

Like a movie.

I realized then that I was dumb. I searched my mind for the right introduction but came up with nothing. I walked to you. Stood next to you at the rail. Looked at the passing meadows and saw nothing.

Hi, you said. I turned. The sun was setting just then, slant light, you were lit from the side. The little down hairs along your arm caught the light.

You were the most beautiful thing that I had ever seen.

If you find this in your backpack, will you write to me?

I'll be in Paris for four days then back to North Carolina.

I think I will always love you.

XO

Dear Love,

Do you remember the walk we took last summer?

We made a nest in the guard house south of the dune.

You, in that half-moon light. You in that dress that god crafted.

Dear god.

I held you and grew warm against your belly. Do you remember?

I tilted your chin and pointed to the sky. Look at that star, I said.

Your eyes drifted up. There were a thousand stars.

What star? you asked.

I made a telescope of my hands and held it to your eye. You adjusted my hands, focusing the aperture.

Oh! I see it now. The bright one, you said.

Yes! That's the one, I said.

Then I tilted the telescope of my hands so your eye was looking at me.

What do you see now? I asked.

Not much, you said. Your eye smiled.

I removed one hand from the telescope, bringing us closer.

Now what do you see?

Not a thing, you said.

I removed my remaining hand and put my right eyebrow on your left eyebrow. Our noses touching.

Now what do you see? I asked.

I shifted my weight.

You breathed deeply.

I reached behind you and pulled you to me. Your back strong through cotton.

The kiss felt like every star come to life.

And in that celestial light, I reviled the most beautiful landscape on earth.

Oh how I miss our summer of salt and sea.

XO

Dear Love,

I've seen you there on the sidelines cozied up inside your big jacket. Despite the layer, you caught my eye and I have been unable to think of much else since.

Sometimes this world seems so cruel and unforgiving. Sometimes this weather feels relentless and heavy. Sometimes, I feel sad about it all.

But seeing you, seeing you smile at me, made me feel alive and well and like love was possible.

I would like to get to know you better. I would like to understand who you are, and I think I would like to love you.

Perhaps we could walk together. I could hold your hand and ask you questions and learn you.

Would you do that for me? Go for a walk. Be next to me?

XO

Dear Love,

I noticed you noticing.

You held my eye as I walked down the aisle en route to 30 D.

I noticed you noticing.

I was flattered, but, in my mind, your muse sat in first class sipping from a glass made of glass. He was thinking of real estate.

Whereas I was thinking of 30 D and feeling prideful that my bag would fit easily under 29 D if the overhead compartment was stuffed. What a pro.

And then I was thinking of eyes and poems.

Eyes held.

Oh, love.

Your deathbed will be much softer if you look through the curtain and find a laptop blazing Excel.

Between you and me, though.

I like the way you rub your palm with your thumb.

XO

Dear Love,

Is this your bag?

Yes, you said. Then you moved your bag to the side.

Thank you, I said.

When I sat, the train station bench creaked. I smiled.

Too many croissants, I said.

I am of slender build, and the comment struck you as funny.

We sat quietly. I took a book from my satchel and opened it.

You looked at my knee.

You looked at my book. I had not turned the page.

Are you looking at my book? I asked.

Your cheeks flushed. Yes.

I closed the book.

You know, you are very pretty, I said.

You tapped your heel on the floor.

I'd like for you to sit with me on the train. We can talk about the book, I said.

Okay, you said.

I picked the book back up and began reading.

I still had not turned the page when the train started to board.

You have not turned the page, you said.

I'm saving it.

For what?

For you.

We did not talk about the book on the train.

I found reason to touch your shoulder by the time we arrived in

Paris.

I'd like to take you to coffee tomorrow. I handed you a pen and paper. Will you tell me where I can pick you up? I asked.

You are very bold, you know.

I know.

You wrote down the name of your hotel.

I'll see you at ten a.m., I said.

You will, you said.

Let us find that moment again, love.

XO

Dear Love,

I read poetry this morning.

Mary Oliver, then Billy Collins, and then the day called my name and said I must go and do something small.

When I stood from my chair, I thought of us. I thought of the poetry of us. It's good. It's a good poem, you and me. One that I return to over and over and always find a new word or meaning that leaves me saying, mmm. Yes. That is true, also.

Our lines match up. You writing yours your way and me writing mine my way and when read together, our lines create something different and good and new every day.

I'm glad to be a poem with you in the morning.

XO

Dear Love,

The basement was a shit show, and I'm glad you gave me that look. The look says, the basement is a shit show, and that's on you.

Now the basement is organized. Look what you can do with one look. Pow. The power of you.

I opened the box of letters before putting it in a better, less shit-show place. I like to look in the box at least once a year. I like to see what started this. Words. Pages of them.

I don't know what you were thinking. Your letters were so beautiful and the writing was so legible and then there was me. It looked like I held the pen with a closed fist. Like a kindergartner. No precision. But there was something in me you saw.

And now, these beautiful letters and these beautiful children and a basement that is not a shit show.

I am thankful for all that can come from a look.

XO

Dear Love,

I knew. I knew in just a moment with you. I knew. I don't know how it works. The knowing. Maybe it's something in my nose and on your skin, or maybe it's something in your eyes that looks like a known thing; ask Freud, ask Jung, don't ask me, all I know is that I knew.

And then I knew again. All over again. That second time seeing you there by the water. You talked about narwhals and islands, and the sun hit you in just the way that it does when it makes knowing bright and clear. I knew then, also.

It feels good to be certain. This life offers little of that. Certainty. But to be certain about you feels like an understanding of gravity or that water is wet. It's very clear.

And even if you don't feel it. Even if we drift, even if the cough is cancer, and I die next week.

I'll know I knew I was certain about loving you.

XO

Dear Love,

Forty years together and my hand still reaches for you in the night. Assurance.

You are there, and I am here, and we are well and safe in this place together.

That is what my touch means.

In that touch, we feel thousands of conversations, experiences, and the sobering moments of reality that have forged this love. In that touch, we find ourselves growing through it all, next to each other, becoming this thing that others may call easy love.

And then we roll to our own sides of the bed. Our own sleeping independent life. All the while knowing that our touch is just there. Assurance.

Thank you, love, for that. For the years it took to find, re-find, and re-find the assurance of living this life in partnership.

XO

Dear Love,

I like to think of us after we've made love. You there in my arms, warm and held and familiar. The sweat of us on my chest and on your back and me not wanting to break that seal.

I like to think of us that way. Sweat. A testament.

I like to think of this while I'm at work. It softens the loud of this place. Maybe someday I'll work in a quiet place. Maybe we will work there together, perhaps on the coast. We could sell whimsical etchings on Japanese fishing floats that we find on the beach. I think people would buy that.

I'm wondering.

I like to think of your strength. The loss you have endured. The sickness you navigated. How strong you must be to knit up your heart and your body and your mind. How strong.

I hope to tell you all this one day. I hope to look at you and tell you how beautiful you are and how your curves feel like known angles.

I hope to tell you how I want to explore all of you.

These strong hands want to be soft and gentle for you. They want to glide over your contours and find your warm places. These hands want to learn and love all of you.

I want to find your scars with my lips and say, I love these parts most.

Until then, I'll stay here, ready and willing. I hope for your reception when the time is right.

XO

Dear Love,

I want to hold you down and explore your body. Take my time. Learn the landscape of your strength and perseverance.

You are life made whole a second time round.

Made stronger and softer by your journey.

I want to run my fingers along all your tender parts. Those parts that make you most alive.

I want to feel myself rising as I run my tongue along the healed parts of you.

The warmth there that speaks to something real and true and whole and you.

Slow and easy, I will slide my hand around your neck, your legs held fast around my hips. I want to feel you deep, now.

Beautiful. Wild.

Hold my eyes with yours, and let us become a new, more beautiful thing together.

XO

Dear Love,

You with those curious eyes and soul searching for truth, for love.

Welcome, I'm glad you are here.

And you there, do I know you? I think I do. It was one, no, two lives ago when we traveled hand in hand to the end of a street in Cape Town. You told me you loved me, then you told me it was time to go. You told me this love would find a home in another life.

Or did I see you at the post office earlier today? Either way, welcome. I'm glad to see you again.

And you, sir, brave sir, with your strong arms and big romantic heart. Hello, comrade. Let us join in brotherhood and put love into this room.

And you, collective you. Beating and pounding and wondering and desiring and yearning and learning and leaning into the evening, let me hold your hand and say yes.

You are beautiful, you are desired, you are loved; I am so glad you are here.

XO

Delight

Dear Love,

I remember falling in love with my babysitter. She was beautiful and kind and had the most lovely hair. I did not know what the feelings were. It was the first time I felt desire. I was six.

I remember running along the sidewalks where I grew up. The sidewalks dipped where driveways came out to the street, and at one dip in particular I would fall and skin my knee. It happened several times. I would cry as my father held me.

I remember a game my sister played with me. She called it doggie. She would crouch down on all fours and I would throw her the candy I had just bought with my allowance. She would retrieve the candy and eat it. I realized when the game was over that I did not have any candy for myself. My sister is smart.

I remember moving. I was so angry that I did not have a say in the matter.

My mom drove the moving van. My job was to say if there were any cars coming when we changed lanes. Despite my anger, I took the job seriously. We did not crash.

Thank you for asking for these memories. I enjoyed sitting at my desk and closing my eyes and thinking about them. Some painful memories came up as well. And some very sweet. Such is life.

XO

Dear Love,

Let me start by apologizing for my disappearance. I know it must have been troubling when you came to wake me only to find a cold bed and my shoes gone.

But I am an adventurous boy and that attribute is not dependent on the clock. Sometimes adventure strikes at midnight.

I awoke with a premonition, and my impulsivity, and penchant for adventure, had me out the door and on my bike before the day had gained five minutes. And now here I am on this train heading north. The ocean is on my left, so north . . . I must be heading north.

I am writing to you from the caboose of the train. I did not know the caboose was still a car that provided value to the railroad, but this train and caboose have some exceptional quality.

The train sparkles. Can you believe that? It sparkles!

What was I to do? Not board a sparkling train just after midnight?

The adventure of it!

At this very moment, I am looking down where the tracks should be, and, well, I don't see tracks at all! We seem to be flying.

I must leave this letter now as there is a knock at the door and I can only assume there is a tiny person on the other side of the door as I can't see a soul through the window and the knocking is coming loud and clear from knee level.

I'll write again as soon as I arrive wherever I am going.

Love to you both.

Your son and brave adventurer,

XO

Dear Love,

A song:

Oh child, oh child, my love is here.

When you feel worried, I am near.

Oh child, oh child, know this to be true.

Always and forever, your Pops loves you.

A story:

There once was a boy, a very kind and curious boy who looked at the world with wonder. The boy was very brave. You cannot be curious without being brave.

Curiosity does not always deliver the answers you think. Sometimes the answers are full of wonder and feel good. Sometimes the answers are scary.

The boy was given a very special gift by his grandfather.

He was given the knowledge that no matter how curious he became, no matter how the world answered his questions, his grandfather would always love him.

Just think of what you will do with your curious mind and the knowledge that you will always be loved.

I'm excited to find out.

XO

Dear Love,

For twelve years, I have witnessed the seasons of you. I've observed the ceremonies you inspire, weddings, renewals, and celebrations of life. I've seen people gathered beneath you in half circles and full circles in support of love.

You always stand proud. Meaning something to everyone. Meaning something.

I've seen you broken. You handle it well. Do you remember the day when it snowed so hard, wet, and heavy that the whole neighborhood was fortified in fallen limbs? You lost a couple of good ones that day. I ran my hands along the rough, cold, lost parts of you.

Now, when I walk to the top of the hill, I make a point to step through your massive split trunks. A holy V that passes me through to the next place of growing. You have born me at least a thousand times: Portal. Threshold. Passage.

But you don't care. You are just growing and living and being.

Today, you wore your leaves heavy. Primed for change. Color filling the tips of you.

Change upon your fingers.

I'd like to write you a book. I'd like to honor your life with a story.

Maybe I should just love you and let that be all.

Beautiful tree.

XO

Dear Love,

I felt your shadow cross over me this morning. Shadow from the half-moon. Just enough light for good hunting.

I had a mouse in my mouth. Its tail curling around my snout as I trotted back to my den. I was thinking only of the urge to retreat before daylight.

I don't know why I feel the way I do, and usually, I don't waste time exploring my thoughts; I just follow their call. It's how I stay alive, I think.

But this morning, your shadow crossed over me, and I glanced up and saw you. You must be seen to be known. You are so quiet. Easy to miss with the ears.

I saw you. You with your wide wings and searching eyes and silent floating twilight.

You had a mouse in your beak as I had one in my mouth. A good hunting morning for you and me. Maybe we are in some ways the same.

How wonderful it must be to hunt from above like that. No hunching or worry of disturbing the dry grass and ruining the prospect.

I sat then, cool dew grass on my haunch, and watched you land on a branch halfway up my den tree. The mouse in my mouth was wet from my breathing. You tipped your proud head back and gobbled down your mouse—the whole thing. No biting or tearing, just a big head-bobbed swallow. What a woman.

I tried to mirror the action but choked on the tail and had to hack up the little mess and eat it in two bites.

You watched. I felt ashamed.

I caught your eye then and felt wholly absorbed in your round knowing. You did not blink for quite some time, and when you did, it only drew me in more—the vanishing and appearing of your eyes like that.

I think you like me. I say this only because you have not looked away, and the bluing sky is stirring up so many opportunities for distraction. But still, you stare at me.

I don't know if it is okay for me to love you. I don't know if it makes sense for my red fur to love your brown feathers, but I feel something stir in me, and it feels like being full. I've never been full, and I like the feeling.

How would it even work, you and me? The mechanics of it. All this fur. All those feathers. I guess we would just need to try and see what came of it.

Tomorrow, I will ease your way. I will hunt you a mouse and plop it down in front of the tree, our tree. I'll make sure it is still a little bit alive so you have the thrill of that living swallow you seem to like.

You amaze me. Ah! Look there, the sun! Let me see you in it. Just a little slice of full-lit you.

Fox

XO

Dear Love,

Ferb (the cat),

The longing never stops.

I thought it would.

I thought, if I could distract myself with the goings-on of my daily routine, the thoughts of your beautiful black coat would ease, and I could get back to my life.

But no. You remain a delicious distraction. I think of that small white tuft of hair on your belly. I think that might be what drew my attention away from the squirrel. Can you imagine! You have the allure to draw my eyes from a squirrel!

The incident has me rethinking my whole existence.

If my love for you is greater than my passion for ridding the world of squirrels, what else may I give up for you?

My tuna?

My rat toy?

My ball of tinfoil?

Yes.

Yes.

Yes.

There is nothing I would not shove under a sofa for you, LOVE.

My beautiful black beauty.

All I do is purr and think of you and let squirrels run by me like a fool. A FOOL!

That is what I have become. A calico fool. A pathetic six-pound mass of soft white, orange, black, and yellow love.

You have done me in.

Today, I will find you a mouse—by god. The finest mouse in this whole damn town, and I will chew it to little bits and leave it for you by your door.

I love you more than wet food.

I love you more than catnip.

I love you more than a wounded bird.

You are the red dot laser that has burned into my heart.

Yours, always and forever,

Felix

(Three doors down)

XO

Dear Love,

Those who look upon me would think I am sleeping. It would make sense for an observer to have such an unassuming thought. I am, after all, lying by the fire with my eyes closed, softly purring into the depths of my cashmere blanket.

Though my body is still, my mind is alight with fantasy and adventure. And at the center of each foray is the thought of you, my perfect winter-coated love.

In my mind, we are walking along the fence that separates my kingdom from the kingdom of dog. We taunt him with our love. The golden bastard.

Look at us, dumb dog, this is what cat love looks like and you will never know it, you stinking, petulant ball of slobber.

Next, I see us sharing a mouse that I expertly captured. I would fillet the little morsel with my pointer claw and let you have the first bite.

Oh my love, how your coat glistens in my mind. You must eat a diet of pure protein and fish oil to achieve such luster.

Now, I turn my thoughts to your ears, those pointed declarations of heaven on earth. Dear god, cat, just look at you.

Little do the idiots know that as I lie here I am planning our future. The names of our kittens will all rhyme. Won't that be cute!

Now I must rise from this glorious vision of us, walk to the human sleeping room, and continue my eight hours of quiet dreaming.

I will see you from the window, tonight.

XO

Dear Loves,

It's 2:00 a.m. and I am once again in that little house behind the big house writing. I'm surprised you never seem to care where I go at night. Now you know. I am, in fact, a writer.

I saunter in here with a lip full of catnip, and I pound away at the typewriter till I get hungry. Then I make that sound you seem to respond to, and one of the big ones of you lets me into the big house.

As a writer, part of my work is to observe. And, dear family, you and those obnoxious feathered creatures you keep in person are what I most observe.

Girl one, I like to watch how creative you are and how much your imagination takes you to interesting places. Just last week I watched you talk at yourself in front of one of those circle reflectors in your room. It seemed like you were in charge of a farm.

I also love how you cuddle me and cover me in blankets. I always know you are watching out for me and I want to thank you for getting that little furry thing for me to look at. I would like to kill it and eat half of it. But . . . I will just look for now.

Boy one, I like how you are so kind to me and how, even though you are very strong, you are gentle with me and let me lie on your furless chest. You don't move even though I know that sometimes you would like to. I also like how you keep the loud one who comes over from picking me up too much. You are very gentle and kind and I thank you for it.

Lady one, you are who I met first and I can't help but think that you chose me to live with you. You gave the evil overlords some of that wallet paper and then they handed me over. It feels like a deal was made. Thank you for getting me out of that evil animal jail.

I want you to know how much I appreciate you and how I notice that you are often gone working. I realize that the Big Stink is around more than you, and that makes me think he may not be allowed with people.

I think you buy my food. I can't think of anything more important than that.

I also want to thank you for coming home and lying down so I can find comfort on your chest. It is lovely to not have a warm flat place to sleep.

Big Stink, I want to thank you for having the largest surface area to lie on. I like that you hold me and care for me. Sometimes I am able to overlook your stink and lie with you. Those are nice times. Also, please stop leaving the writing desk messy. I don't want to clean it up anymore.

I have learned that I love all of you. And if I were ten times bigger I would not eat you unless I was really hungry and we were out of snacks.

XO

Dear Love,

I have learned that when it comes to cats, the best way for them to fall in love is not to care if they fall in love. Cats are drawn to inattention, not that I care.

It's not like I care, but the way you avoid me . . . the way you take the long way round when I lie between you and your destination . . . well, it's hurtful. Not that I care.

I think, and again, not that I care, that if you were to try, at all, to connect with me you may enjoy me and you may find reward in my offerings of attention and my sharing of ball and bone. Not the big bone—that one is mine. But a little bone . . . I would give you a little bone, if I cared.

I try not to care, not that I care. I try to keep my eyes focused on something other than you . . . but Pepper, the way you navigate this world, I find it so alluring. You are able to walk right past a dead seal without rubbing yourself in the putrid delight. I don't know how you do it.

Your self-control is worthy of admiration . . . DEAR GOD, cat, just snuggle me once! Not that I care.

Rub that stupid little nose on my big proud nose, knead my haunch with your fascinating retractable claws, purr in my general direction, swat my ear, SOMETHING, dear god, Pepper, just give me something to let me know you see me and care for me and that if the tsunami came and took the humans that you and I would be okay and we would love each other in a way that would seem very natural under such circumstances and we would form an alliance and I would bring you bits of washed-up fish and you would nuzzle me and I would feel loved . . . I MUST BE LOVED, dear god, Pepper, love me just for a moment, just show me you give a goddamn flea about me, you sleek, beautiful, mesmerizing creature.

Let me lick you and wag for you and let you ride my furry back, you nymph of the night with your big eyes and sneaky, stalky walk. Dear god in heaven, just look in my general direction, PEPPER, love me. LOVE ME.

Not that I care.

Whatever,

XO

Dear Love,

Today the one that feels like love was out. She left me and the one that is loud. I've almost been stepped on twice.

Still, I managed to eviscerate two furry things and one feathered thing, and I have left them both for the one that feels like love to admire before she feeds me.

The one that is loud better not toss them out onto the pine needles before the one that feels like love gets home or I will continue to hate him but with an even deeper quality.

He's not completely horrible, the one that is loud. Just mostly. He comes and goes fast with bangs and stomps and leaves the door open. I like that part of him. The door open part. Sometimes I lie on him or let him scratch me, but it is a favor for the one that feels like love. I know she would like the one who is loud to feel loved.

I know a lot of things about the one that feels like love and the one that is loud. If I'm honest they are my whole life.

I know the one that feels like love is sometimes loud. I know the one that is loud sometimes feels like love. But it's easier for me to distinguish with fewer words.

I know they sit together most nights and listen to things. I know they invite horrible people over for no good reason. I know they go away and I know they come back.

I know they love each other.

I can tell this because they have shown me. You can learn a lot about the pale and furless by watching them.

They will show you what you need to know.

The one that is loud likes to be near the one that feels like love, and I can tell that without her he would be ungrounded and a mess. He has shown me that.

I know that the one that feels like love would feel lonely and listless without the one that is loud.

They keep going, the two of them.

They have taught me that love can be hard. They have taught me that when things are hard you keep going. They have taught me to love even if you don't feel like it. They have taught me that with them around I am safe.

Unless I get stepped on or loved to death.

Now, where was I?

Ah yes! Away I go through the door the one that is loud left open, to kill something for the one that feels like love.

XO

Yearn

Dear Love,

I sat at my piano this morning and looked for you along the beach.

I look for you every year when the tips of the vine maples dip themselves red.

I dream of you most nights. The dreams are not as intense as they used to be. Time has given me that reprieve, but the dreams are warm, playful, and sensual.

I heard a salmon jump as I lingered on the porch with the closing day.

She will head for the waterfall. Our waterfall. The waterfall that opened my heart. The waterfall where I knew I loved you.

Arthur came by to see me yesterday. We attempted to race up the trail to the Kingfisher Lane, but I slipped and damn near rolled into the creek.

He keeps winning. That's okay.

I'm going to play your song now. I wonder if you will feel it all those miles away. Sometimes I think I feel you. Your joy, your sadness. It comes over me. I let myself fall into it, and I feel closer to you.

I may send this letter, or I may add it to the pile of letters in the bottom drawer of my desk.

I still don't know your address. I like not knowing. It keeps you living here.

I'm off to the thrift store now. Thelma's has a new batch of fly rods from an estate sale. Maybe I'll find one for you.

XO

Dear Love,

Today the sea was soft and quiet like a sleeping pup. That's how it looked from the bench.

The day I held you, the sea was a wild animal, a wolf on the run.

Today, the animal of the sea is full.

Out beyond the pointed rock that looks like a birthday hat, there is a gull. He is floating up high, and he does not have a companion. I hope it is the same gull we saw together. The one we named after your last name. The one I said I loved.

Did you know that I sometimes walk along the shore with my eyes closed? I think of you, and I see how far I can get before I walk into the water. Last night I walked a half mile till my feet got wet.

I thought about your eyes. How they catch mine, smile, challenge me, then let me in. I thought about your elbow. I know that's funny, but I like the way you poke me with your elbow.

I thought about touching you, and then I thought about what it would be like to name every bird we ever saw.

That's what I was thinking today when I walked into the water. I opened my eyes and felt wet and alive.

I don't know when I will see you again, but I do know you are right here with me in all the things I see. You are in the birds and pointed rocks and shells.

Everything.

You are right here in the animal of me.

XO

Dear Love,

I woke in the night.

I felt myself moving before being conscious of why.

This hard waking.

My mind switched between two types of imagination. One conscious, the other not. The dreaming of you fueling the wakeful imagining.

This love I have finds you in my wakeful life also. At a distance, I see you in others, the mirage of you, but as the mirage comes closer, it manifests into some other person, and my heart breaks.

Sometimes, I imagine touching your back as you walk by in the kitchen. I kiss you softly, right there, on the nape of your neck. I squeeze your hip playfully and ask your opinion on some pondering. I want you then also. But in a different way.

The hard wakings are visceral. Desirous and as hungry for flesh as I've ever been.

Though the fantasy changes, I always find your lips just there under mine. Your eyes, those eyes of yours, looking into me deep and warm, asking me to give everything I have. Saying you will hold it. All of it. Drinking in everything I am. All of me. Nice and easy.

The only way for me to find sleep again is to play the desire through and release the tension into the night.

Then, I lie in the dark, cooling. Breathing deep and feeling close to you. I don't move. Moving will find you missing.

I want to stay in this conscious glowing until the chance that dreaming will find you again.

XO

Dear Love,

I've been walking in the mornings. A hard fast clip. I leave everything other than my clothes at home. No phone, no watch, just me and my thoughts.

I'm going for a walk with you, that's how I think about it. I feel close to you when I walk. I try to match the pace we kept when we walked through Paris. You were on a mission, and I felt like luggage with a broken wheel. I was doing my best to keep up.

That's how I feel now. Doing my best to keep up. But it's my heart, not you, that is racing me through the streets. My heart holds a sense of urgency at your absence. It races to you and it's all I can do to fill in the steps behind.

When we caught the train, in Paris, you took my hand. You held it hard and said, see, we did it. We can do anything we want. I smiled. You put your head on my shoulder, and as the train pulled from the station I knew I loved you.

That's the moment I most often relive on my walk.

The knowing. The full-body knowing.

I've never been more certain of anything.

XO

Dear Love,

I reached my hand out to you last night. I was lying in bed and I stretched my arm to find you. I like the warmth of you there. The reassurance of your body only inches from me.

All I found were cool sheets. I had to remind myself that you had gone. That you were back on the island and I here in the city.

I could hear traffic outside as the city ramped to a hum, and then I wondered what you were listening to. The wind, perhaps? Something quiet and soft and of the island.

I thought then of the places we both love. The people and communities we have built. I thought of how the missing of us means the having of familiarity, and how the having of familiarity means the missing of us.

Perhaps we can be that familiarity for each other? I don't expect to fill the space of a whole island, just as you are a man and not a city, but for me, we are enough to try.

I want you with me. I want your arm just there under the covers, and I want the reassurance of your voice near me.

Let us try, love. Let us try to be the city and the island for one another. I don't care if it is I on your island or you in my city. As long as it is your body near me when I wake in the night.

Let us try, love.

XO

Dear Love,

I would like you to know that a broken heart is a good thing.

I was walking along the beach at low tide today, and I stopped, as I often do, at the tide pools by the big rock at the south end of the cape. I like to stop there at low tide and peer into the pools near the rocks.

When I look closely I can see a thousand lives playing out. I see barnacles licking at the water for food. I see sculpins chasing each other, hoping to mate, I'm sure. Today I saw a hermit crab looking for a new shell. Her old one had become too small; it was time for her to make a choice.

I watched her for a while. Naked without her shell, vulnerable to attack. She needed to be very careful while she looked.

I watched her try on new shells. I watched her reject most of them. And, in some cases, she was rejected by a shell that was already occupied, filled with sand, or broken in some way.

Eventually, she found just what she was looking for and was made safe and able to grow fully in her new home.

Had she never left the familiarity of her old shell she would not have been able to grow.

This breakup, this being forced from one shell, is exactly what needed to happen.

There will be a shell even more meant for the you that you now are. Don't rush the raw searching. You will be more alive with the right fit.

XO

Dear Love,

The moments we had filled me with such recognition that I will never again know what it is like to be unseen.

That is what you have given me. We recognized each other as sharing the same metaphysical particles. Our thoughts, movements, and reactions were all shared and made whole by the seeing.

As this break in the quantum field closes, I will take with me the knowledge that true, pure, whole love does exist in the universe.

I am made more whole, more alive, and more grounded in what I had only thought to be true.

You leave me as a known being. And for that, I will forever be yours.

I will see you again in another lifetime.

Until then, we will live together in the elevated loving known self.

XO

Dear Love,

Time is moving me closer to the past. I don't know how this is
possible, but each day that passes brings more warm memories from
the summer we spent together.

I like to draw a bath and lie in the warm heat and think of each
moment we had. The soft touch of your hand, the laughter that felt
like home, the feeling that I was not alone. The feeling that I was
more seen than ever.

You do that to me. Light up this life of mine. Even more now, if that
is possible.

In the cool of this winter, I return again and again to the heat of
everything that was our time together.

I don't know if we will relive that experience, but I do know that it is
always with me and always will be, and I am better for it.

You warm me. Do you know that? Even these years later.

I want to reach my hand through time, grab ahold of the us that was,
and pull us right here into the tub with me.

Thank you for the summer of love and the lifetime of feelings.

You are the best summer of my life.

XO

Dear Love,

I climbed the eastern route to the lookout yesterday. The same one we visited last summer before sunrise. The same one where we made love against the granite rock at the base of the tower.

You laughed and held me even tighter when the light came over my shoulder and found your eyes. You sounded nothing but wild.

Animals, we became.

Today is the first time I've been back to the lookout since last summer. I put my hand there on the rock. I leaned into it and tried to send the feeling I had to you over in Europe. I looked at my watch. It was 7:00 a.m. my time. 4:00 p.m. your time. I wonder if you felt what I sent. Did you?

I hope to see you in October when you return from your adventures, but I'm not sure if that will happen. I'm guiding in the Bugaboos through September, then I'm off to New Zealand in November to visit Jon and his crew of misfits. We may just miss each other.

Can we revisit the lookout one day? I hope so. I hope very much so.

XO

Dear Love,

Let me start by saying: you are beautiful. I want you to know how very true that is. I want you to know that you are strong, resilient, and able to navigate the rough water of this life.

There is a kite that is stuck thirty feet up a Sitka spruce at the south of the beach. I've been watching it since June, and here it is December and there it is still stuck.

We have had a number of storms run through this fall, and some of them ripped branches from the low end of the tree. But that kite. It just danced along with it all.

Yesterday the sun came out for a short while and I took it as a sign to go for a walk. I went down to the creek and looked up at the kite.

I saw a small rip near the tail, and the fabric was wearing thin. Just as I was looking at the kite the sun shot through the red and blue fabric and the damn thing looked radiant. It looked divine!

The weathered places let the light shine in a way that made the kite seem iridescent and alive.

You will struggle. You will hurt. You will feel worn. And you will be made even more beautiful because of it.

Give yourself grace. Move with the wind. Let the sun shine through.

XO

Dear Love,

I wonder if you felt it. You must have.

I saw a reaction. Just a moment of hesitation in your being. That was the moment of recognition.

I felt it before I even saw you standing there. A full-body awareness of the lives we have lived. It made me want to cry. They were good lives. Very good.

Then, in that moment I caught your eye, I know you felt it also. In that moment I was washed over with a lifetime of memories. Or the feeling of memories. The feeling that memories make just before you see them in detail.

Then the memories came to me also. I remembered seeing you for the first time, first time, first time. Not this time but the first, first time. It felt like this. Like maybe we had always been lighting and lighting for thousands of years.

I felt your hand in mine. I felt tears from something we had both lost. I felt the transcendent power of our lovemaking. Lost in your eyes, and your eyes, and your eyes, for all the times and lives in which we had felt love and made love and lost and gained.

As you walked past me en route to the bookstore perhaps, maybe to the grocery, I stood for a moment on the sidewalk and felt thankful to have been reunited. If only for a moment. It was nice to love you again. As I believe I always have.

I'll see you soon. I'll always see you soon.

XO

Dear Love,

There is a place I like to go and think of you. I know it sounds crazy, and perhaps I am a little crazy, but I built a place of adoration. I hope to show it to you one day.

It's at the south end of the beach by the creek. I stacked stones in a semicircle so when I sit in the little nook all I can see is the ocean.

The rest of the world, and the wind, are held out.

I sit on the sand there and close my eyes and find you. I trace your face in the sand with my finger.

You and I both know I'm not much of an artist, but tracing you helps me feel close.

I run my finger over your brow, then I round your cheek. It feels like I am with you, and I like that feeling.

I think of you smiling at me. The way you do just after I've tried to make you laugh. It's the smile that I'm actually after, and you always reward me for my efforts.

Do you know how lucky we are to have found each other, at last? Thinking of it brings me joy and peace no matter how big the sea or wild the wind.

You, love, are so very beautiful, and I hope to be with you again soon. I'll show you this place. I'll show you how I trace your most beautiful parts.

XO

Dear Love,

I've been watching the rain through the north-facing window in the living room. The window where we found our reflection as we held each other by the fire.

You fit so nicely in the nook between my chin and collarbone, and looking at our reflection felt like witnessing something complete. Something made whole.

If I close one of my eyes and squint just right, I can see the blurred edges of my face, and I can pretend that you are still here filling the space under my chin. I like to think of that. I like to feel you there.

In the moment of holding and being held by the window, you taught me that love could feel transcendent.

Holding you felt like being held in space with nothing pulling from any direction.

You allowed me to be who I am, and you loved me for it. I've never had that feeling before.

You introduced me to something so true and real that I no longer have to wonder if it exists. I no longer have to wonder if I believe.

You taught me how to receive love. And that is the most precious gift.

I'm going to watch this rain a bit longer. I'm going to hold you in my mind.

I am going to love you some more.

XO

Dear Love,

When I think of New York, I think of all that has changed. I think of the new restaurants and remodeled buildings. Old things re-envisioned and made new. I have learned that there are things that always change.

I have also learned that there are things that don't change. They operate on a different plane than the physical, and this plane, this other place, is where you live in me.

You taught me this.

When I saw you again after all those years, I learned in that moment that warmth and love hold true despite the changes in the world.

I think of how beautiful you were when you greeted me in Santa Maria. I think of how, again, I felt what I had felt when we first met. A soul feeling. A reuniting of something sacred.

I don't know if I will see you again, considering the miles between us. I don't know if there will open up a space for us to be together again in the way we were. The wonder of it makes me ache.

I've learned to love the aching. It says I am alive. It says I am human, and that you are important to me. We are still connected, you and I, and we always will live in the light and desire and love of the moments we shared. And that makes me feel happy.

This time we get to live is so short. I am so very glad that we got to spend some of it together.

How lucky I am to know you.

XO

Dear Love,

I want you to know that you are going to be okay. I want you to know that on the other side of this pain, there is a future worthy of hope.

Your work now, your very heavy work, is to stay open to the possibility of an unexpected future that will bring you joy.

This mountain you are climbing is steep. There will be days when it feels almost unbearable. But those steep slopes will define you.

One day, three years from now, you will go for a walk and you will feel the tender spots and the raw spots and you will realize that the difficulty of this world has softened you into a more compassionate and loving soul.

Compassion for yourself, your children, and those you love.

You did not ask for this part of your journey, but you are being asked to keep going. In time you will find a future that is true, that is yours, that is beautiful.

XO

Dear Love,

I like the coffee here. I like this café.

The seat near the window is my favorite, and I've never found it occupied. It's as if it is meant for me.

I like to watch the people walk by. I think of where they might be going and how lovely and horrible their lives must be.

In my watching, I am only half interested in them.

If I am honest with myself, what I am doing is looking for you.

I know you are out there, and I think I may find you passing by this café one day, though I don't think fate will give me you that easily.

I think I will have to work to find you.

I do know, however, that I will find you.

I like to picture us here at this little table. Knees touching. You with your hands in mine.

I wonder what you are doing now. I wonder if you are looking for me. I think you are.

We will find each other one day, love. I know that to be true.

And what a reunion it will be.

I will hold you.

I will fill you.

We will burn bright, again.

XO

Dear Love,

I'm writing this letter by candlelight.

The flicker of flame is from the candle you bought in Japan. You took it from your travel bag and stuck it in the glass candleholder on my desk. You had to dig out the wax from the last candle with your nail. I liked to watch you do that.

You opened my desk drawer, the third drawer down on the left side, found the matches, and lit the candle.

You are good at that. Knowing how to find the things I've tucked away.

I remember liking how the bottle of cabernet looked when I set it in front of the candle.

The light made translucent red patterns that rolled across your chest.

You in that soft light of fire and wine.

I'm thinking now of how I pushed the papers from my desk, sat you down upon it, then kneeled in front of you on the carpet. I was surprised when I felt the wax dripping down my back.

I remember your laugh from above. You still held the candle when I stood and pulled you to me.

The lamp fell from the table when you reached out to steady yourself. I don't plan to fix it.

I hope your travels bring you back to me. Please replace this candle with another.

XO

Dear Love,

I think about you every day.

I wonder what you are doing and I wonder what you are thinking about. Oftentimes I think about small moments from your childhood.

I feel warm when I think about you, and then I feel loss. I feel a loss for the bond we shared.

You are a very brave and independent woman. I love that about you. I'm proud of that part of who you are.

I think sometimes you are more independent than I am. Perhaps you are more easily on your own. I don't know.

What I do know is that I love you.

What I do know is that I miss you.

What I do know is that I am so very proud of the woman you have become.

I am reminded daily how short and fragile life is.

It's in that fragility that I ask for your understanding.

My choices are my own as yours are your own.

I know I have made choices that seem selfish to you, but the reality is we only get one life. I've tried to live mine as well as I can.

I hope to grow close with you again one day. In the meantime, I'll be loving you deeply, as always.

XO

Desire

Dear Love,

Close your eyes for a moment. Take a deep breath.

That's very good.

Now, imagine yourself lying naked under a thin white sheet. You can smell the sandalwood candle and you can feel the light touch of the blindfold along the bridge of your nose.

Now it is quiet. Just the sound of your breathing into the dark warm space where you lie.

Allow yourself to be discovered. Each small part of your body.
Feel the light touch of my fingers on your collarbone. Just enough pressure to feel my presence.

Feel my hand above your heart.

Now the pressure around your ankles. My hands holding tight, placing your feet six inches apart.

That's right.

Now turn your head to the right. Very good.

I am going to tell you a story. And I want you to listen with your entire body.

Feel this story. Feel the heat. Feel alive and free and desired.

XO

Dear Love,

Do you remember when it rained so hard that the power flickered and went out? We sat on the couch by the fire and listened to the rain through a new quiet. It was just the rain then. The heater had snapped off and with it the mechanical whir from the furnace room.

Stay here, I said.

I returned moments later and made a nest in front of the fire. You watched me at work while you sipped at your tea. I could feel your eyes on me.

Come here, I said.

You stood then and walked to me. The light from the fire jumped and created shadows across the front of your sweater.

Stand here, I said.

You stood where I had pointed. I felt my body responding.

I smiled then.

I walked to you and kissed you softly just below the jaw. I brushed hard against where you are soft. You liked that. The physical recognition of your effect on my body.

I circled you once then held on to your hips and pulled gently. Your underwear slid down with your pants.

I followed your pants to the floor, pulling each of your ankles through the sweats while you put a hand on my shoulder for balance.

I stood again and looked at you there.

Don't move, I said.

You did not move.

I spanked you hard enough to leave a mark. I watched the welt rising in the firelight.

I reached to the front of you and teased your clit lightly then brought my fingers to my mouth and tasted you.

I slid your sweater over your head and looked at you naked.

You are beautiful, I said.

You are beautiful.

You are beautiful.

You are beautiful.

I positioned your hands on the hearth above the fire.

You leaned forward and held the hearth.

I touched you softly from behind.

Don't make a sound, I said.

You tried not to make a sound.

When I slid just inside you, you took a loud breath.

The spank was hard.

I said not a sound.

You nodded.

I took your braids in my hand and pulled back so your chin was forced up.

Would you like me inside you now? I asked.

You tried to nod.

I teased you.

Would you like me inside you now?

You arched your back and brought your hips closer to me.

Your body saying yes.

XO

Dear Love,

You did just what I told you to. You pleased me.

I hope the welts on your ass heal well. I'm sure they will.

I know it's hard for you to let go of control. I'm glad that you trusted me well enough to do just as I said. Your compliance pleased me.

You tested me once. I had to discipline you. I made it clear that you were not to move as I watched you. Just breathing, I said. If I see a knee move, a leg move, an arm adjust, I will stand you up. Turn you around, bend you over the bed, and slap your ass hard enough to leave a mark.

You did move, didn't you. Your naked body edged just a bit as you sat on the bed.

I told you to stand. You stood. I told you to turn. You turned. I told you to lean forward. You did.

I like how quiet you were when I struck you. Then after, when I iced your rising welt, I liked how wet you became for me.

I teased at your shallows then. Just light touches. I could hear you breathing deeply as I circled your clit.

Then, just before you came, I stopped.

I turned you. Sat you back on the bed. I opened your legs with my knee. I leaned you back and brought you to pleasure with my fingers. My hand round your throat.

How lovely it was to spend an evening with you.

Till we meet again,

XO

Dear Love,

There is a long road between the city and the ocean. It goes from four lanes to two. From tall buildings to tall trees. There is a stretch of that road just over the coastal range where it runs straight and true. It's a stretch of road where my mind wanders.

I think of your warmth and your kindness. I think of the loving way you look at the world and how lucky I am to be a part of that world. It is a gift. To be wanted by you.

I think of the angle of your shoulder. How it rounds strong and smooth to your arm. I think of your collarbone and how it feels under my lips.

I think of how you move. Your hips womanly and strong. I want to hold them. I want to watch you move on me. Your sarong pulled up enough for your legs to straddle mine. Look how beautiful you are. Look.

This stretch of road is empty today and the two lanes provide enough privacy for me to reveal my desire. To set myself free as I think of your hips. To glide my hand as you might.

I know this is not advised, and I can only imagine my explanation to the patrolman if I were to wrap this truck around a tree, but the desire for you is so strong and asks for relief.

In my mind, we switch positions and I am between your legs now from above. Your long hair splayed across your breasts. Sweat is there on your forehead. I kiss at it. I want to taste your sweat. I've lost myself in you. Deep and warm and full.

What a mess of me we have made. A sixty-mile-an-hour mess. Old growth whipping by in a blur.

Now, back to this driving, back to this driving.

Yours,

XO

Dear Love,

You did just as I asked and I was very pleased with you.

You sat as directed, you ate as directed, and when I told you to spread your legs under the table so I could tease you with the cool rounded handle of the dinner knife, you obeyed.

But now, here in the hotel, when I asked you to fetch me a glass of ice, you returned without ice.

You like to test me, don't you? You like to see if I'll follow up? If the consequences are real.

I spanked you hard, three times. Your ass beautiful with the welt rising. Then I pat the bed. You sit.

I spread your legs and wet you with my mouth then buzz at you soft with the vibrator.

I find a rhythm and watch your breathing speed as I add pressure. Your nipples hard. Your wet rolling slow.

Your breathing quickens. I keep my pace. I watch your jaw tighten. Then I pull the vibrator from you just before you come.

You will fetch my ice, next time, won't you, love.

You catch your breath.

Yes, you say.

You return with my cup full of ice and again I lean you back on the bed. I put a piece of ice in my mouth then tease your clit with it.

Stay quiet for me, love. You stay quiet.

I slip the ice inside you and watch it melt. A beautiful little puddle.

Then I warm you with my heat. Deep and full.

This time, I let you come.

XO

Dear Love,

When I think about us, and the potential of us, and the impossibility of us, it leaves me aching.

The ache is worth it.

My love for you and the wild ease and depth of our connection is a reward worth the pain of our distance.

If we met, and that seemed impossible, perhaps this world will bring us together again in a way that does not ache and does not leave us wanting more.

The love I have for you appears in the small moments.

A touch from you, a message from you, a smile.

Those small things make me feel your love and our connection. I am thankful for those soft moments.

I am thankful also for the sensual moments. The fullness of you inside me. The growing of you at my touch. The tease of you and how my body responds. Heating and opening for you.

I love how you move in me. The safety of you and the power of your body in mine brings me to a sensual awareness outside of myself.

The uniting of flesh and soul feels transcendent.

You are an incredible lover. I love to hear your calm breath as you ease your stride, having emptied yourself and having filled me. I love how you hold me in the dark.

Sometimes I wonder if this distance is why we work. If the mystery and the almost having of each other keeps us bound.

I don't know. I don't think so. I think the bond we share is deeper than the miles, and I hope that our lives can be made more whole by the potential of being close, the potential of the impossible made possible.

We found each other, and perhaps one day, we will find each other ever closer.

Until then, I ache for you. And I welcome the depth of what that means.

You are worth the miles.

XO

Dear Love,

The knock was expected.

I felt heat flash through my body. First in my belly, then up to my chest. Then down. Like a wave.

You knocked again. I opened the door, and in the dim light you looked older than I knew you to be.

My nervousness caught in my throat. My salutation felt off. I recovered and welcomed you into my room.

The lake was visible through the door, and you turned and told me to look.

We looked at the moon's reflection on the wind-waves. I felt your hand brush mine.

You turned and found my neck with your lips. You moved my hair to the side and kissed your way to my ear.

You were forward. You were gentle. I felt safe.

I did not expect the slowness of you. I thought a younger man would be urgent, but you took your time, and my body felt warm and my breath drew deep with each tease of your lips.

You pushed slowly against me in the doorframe, and I could feel your desire grow against my belly.

Your fingers worked slowly at the button of my jeans. My pants loosened and you pulled them down. You paused before slipping them over my ankles and kissed the scar on my belly just above my underwear. You looked up then and caught my eyes. Your eyes were kind and hungry.

Then you kissed me soft on my thigh as you pulled my pants free.

I became conscious of the scene. The little cabin near the lodge. I could hear music from the lodge and wondered if someone standing on the porch could see us. I don't think so. It was a ways off and the night was dark.

You rose to find my lips, and your fingers brushed at my softness.

You put your foot between my feet and eased my legs open. Lips on my neck again, soft. Your fingers moving so slow. Teasing.

I did not expect my reaction. I pulled your hand from between my legs and slipped your fingers into my mouth, then I instructed you to slip my underwear to the side. You did as you were told.

It was in that moment that I realized that you, a beautiful young man, were desiring to please me. You were a fantasy come to life, and I was not going to miss the opportunity to explore my desires.

Slowly, I said. As your fingers dipped just inside me. Slowly.

You obeyed.

Visit me again, love, at the lake.

XO

Dear Love,

I touch myself. Gentle. Feeling myself warm. Feeling my body prepare for you.

I bet you are thinking of the day ahead. I bet you are scheduling something. I like to think of you working. Solving the world's problems . . .

My body rising more now. I like to pretend your body is on mine. Warm and moving. I like to pretend I am looking at us from the door. My legs are wide for you. Open for you. Your strong back flexes as you move.

I like that. Picturing us. I pull my underwear to the side and find myself ready for you. I glide my fingers as you would. I arch my back a little. Just so. Yes, just so.

I like to feel my body ready itself for you. I like to bring myself to the edge of release. Then I like to ease away. Wait. Pulse. Wait.

Come home to me, love. Come home and fill me with heat and strength and everything you are.

XO

Dear Love,

The blindfold was tied in such a way that when you leaned back you could see a sliver of my movement in the firelight. Nothing more.

You could only see pieces of me. My forearm. Wet from the bath. A bubble caught the light. The bubble moved when the muscles in my forearm moved. You like my forearms. They are strong from work in the garden.

You heard the fire crack and spit and adjust itself with the log I had added, and then you felt the water stir as I stepped back into the tub.

My fingers pulled the blindfold down. Then you saw nothing.

No peeking, I said.

Okay, you said.

I sat then in the bath and you felt the water rise up your chest. I tucked my legs between yours.

You felt my hand around your ankle.

I like this part of you, I said.

Thank you, you said.

I pulled your left ankle from the water and set it on the rim of the tub.

I lathered my hands and slid them around your calf.

Everything was dark. My hands felt warm.

How do you feel? I asked.

Weightless, you said.

You noticed the strength of my hands. You noticed the heat of the water.

You noticed the crack of the fire and the tap of rain against the window.

The night is ours, I said.

Okay, you said.

You heard the faucet. The water warmed as my hands found your thigh.

My love, I said.

Yes, you said.

When you return, I'll draw a bath for you again.

XO

Dear Love,

I find you there under the sheet.

I trace your thigh with my finger till I find the slope of your hip.

I brush your neck with my lips. A soft kiss there. Then, under your jaw. A kiss there. Soft.

A kiss then again at your neck.

Another kiss there.

Open your legs for me, love.

I trace the inside of your thigh.

Guess what I am spelling.

You try to follow the finger.

I kiss your neck again.

What did I spell?

I don't know, you say.

I trace slowly to the outside of you.

A graze along your lips. Just barely.

I'll try again.

I spell the word on your thigh.

What did I spell?

I don't know.

Open your mouth, love.

I dip my finger in your mouth.

And return to the outside of you.

Tracing a wet line around you.

Then dip slowly just there.

I try the word again on your thigh.

You nod.

And spread your legs wider.

XO

Dear Love,

I took your hand and led the way.

When we entered the room you let go of my hand and closed the door.
You pushed me soft against the door. I felt the cool of the wood along
my spine. You kissed my neck, breathed deeply, and then whispered,
Stay.

You walked to the bed and pulled the covers back, exposing the cool,
crisp sheets.

You were fluid in your movements, and with each preparation my
anticipation rose.

The play of power felt balanced as you did what I asked of you and
then I did what you asked of me. Our exchanges seamless.

When you returned to me I found your lips again and pushed at your
shoulder till you sat on the bed.

You watched patiently while I removed my earrings, bracelet, and
necklace. I put them on the nightstand and then pulled your shirt up
and over your head.

Your shoulders were round and strong, and the youth of you struck
me. Your neck was tan and unweathered, your chest strong and
unconvinced of gravity.

I reached down, unzipped your jeans, and released you.

I slid to my knees and slid you into my mouth.

Your sounds made me hungry to hold you firm in my hand and then
later inside.

XO

Dear Love,

You lay on the table breathing in deeply the scent of mint, sage, and lavender. The night was warm, even for late spring, and sweat ran down your chest as you waited for my next instruction.

Good, I said. Now, close your eyes.

You did as you were told.

Now, take yourself in your hand.

You reached down and found yourself curiously hard given the circumstances.

I walked around the table and dripped warm oil on your stomach. I chanted as I walked past your head. You grew harder yet.

Move your hand with my voice, I said.

You did as instructed and slid your hand along in time with my chant.

You felt weightless and soon the table was no longer supporting you.

As you rose above the table I removed my cloak and straddled your hips.

Now, give me your hand, I said.

You reached your oil-slick hand to me and I held it with strong fingers.

I chanted louder as our bodies merged. I felt wet and wild and alive. I chanted louder as your hips moved. You felt me clench on you as your release met mine.

All the candles in the room blew out at the sound of my ecstasy. The wind howled as I took you in. I filled myself with your soul. As you eased back to the table, I held inside the power of both of us.

The night was young; the other men sat quietly in their chairs. By daybreak, I would rule them all.

XO

Cherish

Dear Love,

I find you everywhere.

I find your hat on the rack by the door. Your bracelet on the dresser. Your little messes of feathers and rocks in the mudroom.

I don't know what to make of it other than to say I like the feeling of it. You here. In this place.

I see this child growing inside you. Your belly taking the form of a home. I hope she is mine. And I hope you will let me love her.

I don't know why you won't tell me.

Tracy called it out when you arrived, and I saw the change too. Your body employed with overtime work. I saw the round of your cheeks and the swelling curves through your tee shirt. You looked radiant.

I don't know if you will stay or go or if you will tell me or not. I don't feel inclined to ask. It's up to you whether I get to be a part of her life.

I don't know why you would want me to be part of anything. Me, the bedraggled. Me, the struggling owner of the struggling bar, betrothed to the bank and the government.

I have not known much to be certain in this life. It all seems up to interpretation, and god knows I've interpreted it a thousand different . ways.

But I have not done that with you.

Even the first time. When we were floating on warm red wine, even then, I knew.

Even then I knew, in the haze, the teeth, the nails, and the sounds of your reception. Even then, I knew I loved you.

If you leave, take some of me with you.

Whatever you want. You can have it all.

XO

Dear Love,

Sit with me here and watch the leaves fall. I like to be near you.

My leaf will surely land on the deck before yours. If we tie, I will let you win. I'm working on that. Humility.

I like starting the day like this.

You next to me.

The coffee a little too hot.

We will need to drink it slow and we will need to spend that time close together.

There are moments like this when I think how all of life has created the context that makes now, just now with you, so perfect. I would not want to be anywhere else. That is one thing I know for certain.

When the coffee is gone and we have washed our cups and set them to the side of the sink to dry, I will lean into you. You will do the same. *Yes*, our bodies will say.

Not even 11:00 a.m. and the day has been made.

When we return from the bath we will towel dry by the fire. You will tease me for missing a button on my shirt.

Then we will walk the lane to the creek.

You in that fleece that I love. Me in my wool sweater that you say makes me look like a poor professor.

I will be poor with you. I would not mind.

There is nothing in the world that I would rather do than live in this way with you.

XO

Dear Love,

This morning was cold. Clear and cold. I walked along the reservoir, and as I made the left turn by the big fir tree, the one you said reminded you of me, I felt warm.

I realized in my body before my mind that I was thinking of you. You do that. Warm me.

In that warmth, I assembled a vision, and the clarity and the heat of it had me smiling wide. I must have looked like a fool walking that last quarter mile with a lover's grin.

I hope I do the same for you. I hope you can find warmth in me and in the memory of what we held together.

Sometimes I think of your touch—the tips of your fingers on my cheek. I think of the care I could feel even with that small physical connection.

There is safety in you.

When I reflect on what is most precious to me in this life, it is the feeling of love, safety, and adventure.

You give me all three. I hope I do for you also.

With warmth on this cold day,

XO

Dear Love,

Be with me now. Let me hold you and move your hair behind your
ear and be tender with you. I'll whisper a story in your ear. A story I
have not told you. Not because I did not want to tell you but because I
am just now remembering it and I want to keep you here. Warm and
open and listening.

There was a coyote with a very short tail that used to trot along the
beach. He was proud. So proud that he skipped more than trotted. He
looked to be enjoying his walk, and whenever a seabird would swoop
toward him to take a closer look he'd shake his nub tail with pride.
I'm still here, he would say. I am still here. There is so much left of
me. He was proud of his short tail. He was proud of his survival.

Why did you tell me that story? you ask. I kiss your ear. I told you to
keep you here. I wanted to entertain you. I wanted to be warmed by
you and I wanted you to know that loss can be something to be proud
of.

I think you are very strong. I think you will be okay. I think I am
lucky to have held someone like you. I am lucky to have a spirit like
yours so close to me.

I hope you see yourself like I see you.

XO

Dear Love,

It's cold this morning. I have the space heater on full blast, but its usefulness ends at my knees, and everything north of there feels like ice.

Do you remember the cold mornings in the cabin? We were so poor and wanted to save money on heat. We suffered for that. I would not have done it any differently.

On these cold days, I like to think of those cold mornings under the four layers of blankets, under the old cedar shake roof, under the snow, under the big cold sky. Those were some of the best mornings. Warming with you. Our bodies doing work. I would let you put your hands on my chest and I felt so proud when I did not flinch. I let you put your feet on my belly once. Do you remember? It was all I could do to pretend they did not feel like daggers.

I like to be cold with you, I like to be warm with you. I like to share the journey with you. All of the temperatures. All of the feelings. All of me with you.

Sending you love in the cold coming days of winter. I will always be here to warm you.

XO

Dear Love,

This life is short and I see the evidence daily. I'll never be younger than I am now, and I'll never be more able to do what I want to do or say what I want to say.

I want to share something with you. It is something that is very important to me.

There are only a few people in my life that ignite the place in my heart that makes me most human.

You are one of those people. You are someone that my heart has chosen to hold and care for deeply.

I want you to know that I love you.

I'm not asking for it back.

Loving you is enough for me.

I'm glad you know.

Yours,

XO

Dear Love,

Allow me to be tender with you. Let me tell you that you are
beautiful and alive and you are more today than you were yesterday.

This journey you have been on did not begin by choice. You were
delivered to this world and a set of circumstances beyond your
control. This world handed you difficulty and sorrow and mountains
too large for many to climb.

But here you are. You made it. You took circumstance and applied
choice, and you survived and are stronger and more beautiful and
more human because of it all.

I love you when you struggle, I love you when you fail, I love you
when you succeed, and I love you when you thrive.

That is what this next chapter is. Your time to thrive. You are the
hero of your story. You are a survivor, a wild adventurer, a beautiful
soul, and this world is better because of who you will become.

XO

Dear Love,

These cold days have me feeling reflective. I walk down the sidewalk here on Fifty-Fifth and think about life and where I am taking it.

Other times I walk down the block and look at all the houses and think about all the stories unfolding there. Stories of love and drama and heartache and success and hope. Always hope.

Sometimes I look at your house and think of the love there. I think of the struggle also and the thousands of things I don't know.

What I do know is that the house over there, across from me, the yellow one, is full of care, love, and perseverance. I see it in your advocacy for your children, in your loving partnership, and in your never-ending pursuit of making things just a little better for everyone.

Have you tried walking barefoot? It grounds you. Have you tried ChatGPT? You can get so much more done! Have you tried aromatherapy?

You are an amazing woman and I'm happy to have you in the forty-five club. You will continue to do wonderful things in this world, and even more importantly, you will continue the pursuit of making things just a little bit better for everyone.

I think you are wonderful.

XO

Dear Love,

I don't trust easily. In fact, most people feel fear when they see me. I pick up on that and I fear also. When I feel fear I show strength. It scares people. The strength of me. And when they leave me alone I feel safer.

I've never felt that way with you. Even when we first met I sensed something in you that brought me comfort. You felt known.

I tested you. I wanted to be sure my instincts were right. They usually are. I was not wrong about you.

Each day that you showed up for me became proof that you could be trusted. I learned that you were strong. Like me.

I learned that you were formidable. Like me.

I will always give you what is true. As you have given me what is true.

I don't need to guess with you, and to me, that means everything.

You have learned me. You have listened to me. You have not judged me.

I feel that.

Something special happens when like discovers like. That is what has happened to us. We have a shared spirit.

We are wild.

We are loyal.

We are strong.

XO

Dear Love,

Do you know how beautiful you are? I hope you do. And I hope you can feel deeply what I see.

Do you know that I love touching you? I love the heat of your skin and the softness of your neck. I love the arch of your collarbone. You ignite my senses, and my body responds in a way that brings desire warm and steady, then in an aching surge.

Through you, I am made whole and hungry at the same time. Your thoughtful way and quiet observation of the world bring me peace. And in that peace is a love that I have never before known.

XO

Dear Love,

I have lived many places, but none of them felt like you.

I have felt grounded.

I have felt comfortable.

I have felt safe.

But with you, I feel all those things at once, and there is no other word for that ease than *home*.

This home, this you, was unexpected, like looking for a sip of water and finding a lake.

That's what you are to me, a wide-open clear pool.

I love the clarity of you. Knowing that what I see is what there is. Your openness has allowed me to view your depths, and still I want only to know more.

I hope to spend a lifetime discovering the warm, clear connection we share.

XO

Dear Love,

Tonight, when you close your eyes, I want you to take a deep breath and say out loud:

I am beautiful,

I am beautiful,

I am beautiful.

Even if you don't believe it, even if you squirm at the idea of it. Do it anyway. Say it.

And then tomorrow, when you wake, say it again.

I am beautiful,

I am beautiful,

I am beautiful.

Then, if even for a moment, open your soul and try to feel the words deeply.

I think you are beautiful. I think the nature of your living, feeling, and hurting makes you beautiful, and your work is to think that also.

I believe that we find what we are looking for. Don't you?

If you commit to the journey of looking for your beauty, your worth, your special way of being in this world, I am sure you will find it.

Until then, darling:

You are beautiful.

XO

Dear Love,

The morning filled itself up more quickly than we thought, and now here it is noon already and time to eat and time to think about the afternoon and time to begin managing the next and the next and the next thing.

How quickly it all slips by. I think this world would like all of your attention. I think this world would gobble it up, smile, and ask for even more. But there is just one you, and this world is very large and very hungry.

Today, love, I would like for you to give to this world in an even more profound way than what it is asking from you. I want you to show up to this world with your gift, your attention, and your words. I know you can. And now, love, you must.

There are so many asks of you. This is an ask from you. Prioritize her. She is beautiful and she has a gift to share.

Twenty-five minutes today and tomorrow and the next and the next, for you and your words. You don't need to put a word count on it. Giving your gift must be a habit, and habit is not about speed.

The spark is there, love. Fan it, protect it, give it attention, and let the fire burn, then share the light.

I believe in you, and I know deep down you do too.

XO

Dear Love,

Dance with me.

How beautiful you are.

Move your body to the rhythm within and free your wild soul. All of you. All of you.

You are your own today. Yours only. And in that celebration of the whole self, of the whole loving self, you will fall deeper and rise higher into the beautiful light that is your own.

Hold together your hands under the poplar tree. Be clothed in a gown of roses.

And as the sun sets you will alight to a color only seen when the setting sun finds a rose.

You are yours, love.

You are alive, love.

Now lift the elderberry and rosewater flute and taste the beauty of the earth, the beauty that is you, the beauty of this day.

Be nourished in the knowing:

You are wild.

You are powerful.

You are your own.

XO

Dear Love,

There are so many things beyond your art that make you beautiful. And if you were to go through this life with those things only it would be a life worth living.

But when you include your art in your life it makes you radiant. And there is nothing more wonderful than a radiant spirit.

I think part of our life journey is to discover the art that lives in us. Art holds a bit of the divine, don't you think?

Art is being human at the deepest level.

When you read this I want you to say to yourself:

I am an artist.

I am an artist.

I am an artist.

Then, make the time. Twenty-five minutes, at least, today, tomorrow, the next day, and the next to be made full through your art.

Create. And through creation, be made whole.

Doing. Is being.

XO

Dear Love,

I just wanted to know you were there. A little warmth in the dark. I found your arm with my pinky. That's all I needed.

I smiled into the dark. I checked the time. 5:00 a.m., not so early.

It was the time of morning when sleep seemed like something done and waking seemed like something not yet worth pursuing.

I decided to spend the in-between time thinking of you.

This hour is not too early for us, is it, love. Together we have packed our bags, checked our tickets, roused children, clicked into boots and pedals, tied laces, seduced finicky stoves awake, planned our route, unzipped tents to find the dark cold world waiting. And always we have made the next decision together. Do we go? Do we stay?

We mostly go. Don't we.

So many of the most beautiful sunrises I have seen are followed quickly by seeing you. You are the one constant among a variety of landscapes, and even in our own adventures, you are never far from my mind. You are who I want to share the beautiful moments with.

He is loving this.

Or, he would love this.

Those are often my thoughts just after my own adoration of this beautiful world.

Do you know how much I love waking with you? When I wake with you near, I feel certain that the day, no matter how hard, will bring joy.

I don't know how you do it. Honestly. Even in the dark times, you find the will to pretend to be a horse and make the children laugh. Even in the hard times, you manage to make these mornings an exciting possibility for adventure and laughter.

I love you for making this world of ours joyful. I love you for your persistence. I love you for your tender moments along with all that *go* energy.

And I love that this morning my pinky has found you. And in that discovery of you there, I know that today will be another best day of my life.

XO

Dear Love,

I think that one is hungry, you said.

I looked at you and smiled. You wore an earnest expression. Your gaze was set on the white bunny that sat looking at us from the edge of the lawn.

I don't know if he is hungry, I said.

He is! Look at him. He is sniffing the air and looking from side to side. That means he is very hungry!

But look how fat he is, I said.

Just because he is fat does not mean he is not hungry, you said.

Then you reached into the basket and picked out two baby carrots.

Those are mine! I said.

You had already begun to walk toward the fat bunny. My words fell at your heels.

These bunnies spook easily. We had discovered that from previous lunches on this bench. The bunnies scattered whenever I stretched or sneezed, and you would always look at me and shake your head.

You need to be gentle, you would say.

When you walked across the lawn the bunnies did not mind. They felt safe. When you walked to the fat bunny he regarded you with the appreciation of an old friend come to visit.

You handed him my carrots and he plucked them from your finger like a lover's kiss.

I love this about you. I love the ease that you bring to the vulnerable. The care that you hand to the small and the furry.

You are kind. You are beautiful.

You can have all of my carrots.

XO

Dear Love,

The moon rose full and heavy at the ragged edge of the world. She was whole and beautiful, even where the peaks cut her. Maybe even more beautiful there.

Perspective.

They say that the moon is made from the earth. They say that millions of years ago, something large smashed into the growing world and shot wild bits of earth into the heavens.

In time, the bits found each other and made something of themselves.

An explosion can create something new and beautiful. Isn't that lovely to know?

The moon pulls at my desire, especially when it is full.

She pulls at the parts of me that want to be seen and illuminated in the night.

You do that also. I feel known in your warm glow.

I feel the power of you.

Does that make sense?

Like you, the moon does not need me to look at her. She does not need my adoration to be made full and well.

A bright light, all on her own.

Though it sure feels good to be a witness of her rising and to be touched by her light.

XO

Dear Love,

I like to watch you move through the shadows.

Delicate, graceful, strong.

Wild thing.

Move with me now, will you. Sway just a little to the sound of this rain on the window, branch shadows moving us along in their flexing life.

I like to move with you in the way the world asks.

We are doing just as we are meant. We are living just as we must.

Let me look into your eyes for a moment.

I see you there.

I feel you now.

Even in writing this, there is something very powerful I feel. A moment we are sharing. You all the way there and me here.

Stuck will be unstuck.

Purpose will be revealed.

Until then, let us move with the shadows. Let us give and receive.

Let us listen.

Let us know one another.

XO

Dear Love,

The wind was relentless today, but we journeyed on as we always do.

And now, as we bed down with the roll of the sea, I feel a sense of calm.

I love to watch you there at the wheel. I love the way your eyes glance from the horizon to the helm. There is something so sure about you, even in uncertainty.

You do that for me, create surety in uncertainty. How wonderful this life with you has been for me.

I don't think that wonderful can be true without pain. We have had that also. And in some ways, I am glad for it. I know how to love you and I know how to hurt with you, and both those ways of being together have made us closer.

All that beautiful, horrible, wild living we have done. I would not trade it.

And now here we are, continuing our journey on our boat. I'm glad we named her *Spirit*. It's another example of how love and loss can stay with us as a meaningful part of our journey.

Hold my hand, love.

Come what may.

XO

Dear Love,

I am my own. And you are your own.

But together feels like ease. A hand held. At last.

Outside, the curve of the lake disappears into fog.

Here, the curve of your hip disappears under my hand.

You are asleep as I write this. I smell you on me. Familiar. I am glad of it.

Last night, when I woke you with a hand on your back, you edged closer to me, rocked your hips, and felt me wanting.

I've missed you, you said.

Slow and soft was an act of restraint, and when your nails racked my back, it was all I could do to keep from devouring you entirely.

I will make coffee now and place it there on your nightstand.

A slow waking for you.

I like to watch the day find you.

I always have.

Let us warm each other once more.

Then to the lake. Your hand in mine, again.

XO

Dear Love,

When I travel, I like to find a quiet place in a park and sit on the grass. I close my eyes and feel into my body.

I like to see if I can pay such close attention to the world that I can feel the planet turn.

During one such endeavor, I opened my eyes to see a bee just inches from my nose. I watched the bee land on a wild rose. I watched the little back legs stepping up and down, collecting pollen while its straw-like mouth collected nectar.

I wondered how the bee chose that particular wild rose.

The rose was open and in bloom and being itself.

The rose was being a rose.

It's amazing how all creatures seem to do two things at once. Bees collect nectar and serve the great blooming world at the same time.

I think about you and the two things you are doing at once. Moving through the world while giving friendship and love. It's important work, what you are doing.

A spirit like yours will be met.

Your openness and desire to live fully will find its match.

Your job is to open and bloom, and let the world do the rest.

XO

Dear Love,

I adore you. I know I don't say it enough. Words are sometimes hard for me to find.

I think you are beautiful. Not just in the arch of your cheek or the warmth of your smile. I think you are beautiful because of your passionate nature. You are beautiful because of how you welcome the world into your heart. I see your beauty in everything you do for this family.

I am thankful that you have the words for us both. It would be a too-quiet world if I were on my own.

You make me whole.

I find peace when I am lying next to you. Your body and your spirit do that for me. Peace.

Let me tell you now, love, without the shield of quiet protection I have learned to hold, without the grasping at the words that are felt but not shared.

I adore you.

I hope you feel my love through my actions. I hope you feel my love when I fill you in the dark. I hope you feel my love in the small quiet moments we share.

Let me hold you tonight. And in my arms, I hope you find some of what you give to me returned.

In this life, I choose you. And I am so very grateful you chose me too.

XO

Dear Love,

Sometimes when we are in bed and you are sleeping I like to reach out my hand and just lightly touch you. I like to pull my fingers away just a little so that when you breathe the tips of my fingers find you. A light touch at each inhale.

I don't know why I do this. I think I just love knowing you are so close. I like knowing that I could hold you if I wanted to. I like knowing that we have found each other.

I did not know if I would find you. I did not know if I would one day find a love that I could lie next to and almost touch as she slept. It would have been okay if I hadn't. I had resigned myself to living a good life on my own.

But now, now with you just there and me inches from you, I find the joy of this life is made much deeper by your place in it.

I like to navigate this world with you. I like to laugh with you and I like to sit in awe with your hand in mine.

I love to walk near you along the city streets, and most of all I like to know you are here. Breathing and living and being the one I have given my heart to.

XO

Dear Love,

This life is funny, isn't it? Sometimes the future finds us and gives us what we desire. Or, in this case, the past comes back and provides a future we did not expect.

I did not expect you to return to my life. I certainly did not expect you to return into my life holding an offering of love. But now that you are here, and we are reunited, I feel so deeply grateful for what our past is offering to our future.

I love our shared history. I love that we knew each other as young people, and now, I am discovering, I love that we know each other as adults.

I would like to explore this life together. I would like you close and I would like to hold your hand, not in my mind but in this life and into the future.

Sometimes this feels like a Hallmark movie. The reuniting after all these years at a reunion. The spark of interest I could feel in my belly as our conversations developed. And now the missing and wanting you close and wanting to try this life with you more fully. I like this movie we are in.

I was skeptical at first, but now I believe that real-life love stories can happen. It has happened to me.

So, let's try. Let's try to explore this world together. Let's try to be a part of each other's future, not just each other's past.

Perhaps we will make it to the next reunion together. I'd like that.

Together.

Let's try together.

XO

Dear Love,

I held you for some time after. I stayed there inside you and did not move. I breathed deeply with you as my body loosened. Then I slid from you slowly. I did not want to hurt you. I would have stayed there on top of you until I fell asleep, but I was strong and heavy, and the weight of me was a lot to bear. That is what I thought.

That is not what you felt. I know that now. You liked me there on top of you. It made you work to breathe, but that working felt like pleasure. The working felt like assurance. That I was there and I would stay.

When I did ease from your body I draped an arm over your chest. You looked up at the ceiling feeling warm and full and loved.

What are you thinking? you asked.

You like to ask what I am thinking. I am not one to share my thoughts freely.

I am thinking I love you, I said.

Why are you thinking that? you asked.

You liked to push me. You like to get me to say more. I knew you would ask me why. I was quiet as I thought.

I love how I feel when I am with you, I said. I love that we have lived lives on our own and have learned the world and have found each other with the knowing of the world. I love your wisdom. I love the gentle care I see in your eyes. I love the safety of knowing that we are okay on our own but we are better together. I love being here next to you.

You smiled into the dark. Those are good things to love, you said.

Yes, I said.

Let's keep loving each other, you said.

Yes, I said.

XO

Dear Love,

I have watched you navigate this world for many years. I have seen the kindness in your thoughts and the challenges that you overcame.

I have seen you choose kindness. I have seen you choose to love. I most see who you are in that choice. Love.

There you are, I say. There you are, you beautiful soul.

You have struggled and hurt and lost and persevered. This being human is not for the faint of heart, and you, love, have done human very well.

You've let it all come to you and you kept going.

As you lean into trust, the world will open for you. As it has, as it will do.

Each day you are finding an even more beautiful self.

I am glad to know you. I adore you. This world is better with the care and love that you are offering to it.

Today you will live deeper. Today you will love yourself more fully. Today you will give your gift to the world.

Today you will be open to the spirit that guides us all.

XO

Dear Love,

This room is full, for you. The city is made bright by you.

You do that, you know. Make this town full and bright.

You connect us.

Through humor, love, adventure, and friendship.

You connect us.

The spin of the wheel and off we go.

You wild thing.

I don't know where this will land. I do know I will be more human because of it.

Glasses-raised smiles open on a week of worry because of you.

You the bright star that holds the eye a little longer.

I love the constellation of this town. And love, it is better seen because of you.

Your light lands us here, in this place.

And this place is made more beautiful because of you.

XO

Dear Love,

It did not go all at once.

First, there was ringing, maddening ringing; then there was nothing. I preferred nothing to the ringing.

They sent me home when it was gone entirely. It may have saved my life. I did not feel thankful. I wanted to stay and fight.

The first time we met, you taught me how to feel sound. You would place my hand on your throat and hum. I liked the feel of the sound.

Letter writing was your idea. It became my morning ritual, and then, after some months, it became my afternoon ritual as well. We grew a quiet love through vibration and words.

Our love did not feel quiet when I visited you in the city. It felt louder than anything I had ever known.

You lived in that walk-up apartment on Fifth and Pine, and when I put my hand to the wall, I could feel the streetcars pass. During rush hour, we would sit on the edge of your bed, put both hands on the brick wall, and feel footsteps from the sidewalk. I liked to feel the city.

I opened the window on our first night together. The room needed cooling, and I liked the contrast of the cool room and the warm of you.

I found you there under the sheet and traced your thigh with my finger till I found the slope of your hip.

I brushed your neck with my lips. A soft kiss there. Then, under your jaw. A kiss there also. Soft.

I put my hand on your throat and felt the vibration.

A kiss then again at your neck.

I traced the inside of your thigh and spelled a word.

You tried to follow the finger.

I looked at you to see if you knew what I had spelled.

You nodded and drew me in close.

The room was cool in the morning. I thought of streetcars and footsteps.

I thought of old men smiling. I thought about women raising an eyebrow. I thought about shaking heads and the feeling of something like hunger.

I put my hand on your throat and felt desire fill the room.

I thought of those on the other side of the street. Then I held you more firmly at the hips so they would feel you also.

XO

Dear Love,

I have a hard time saying what I feel. We both know this, but what I feel about you deserves a voice, and you deserve to hear it.

For eight years, you have been here with me. Holding me and loving me for who I am, and I hope I do the same for you.

I hope my touch and my desire are able to help you feel some of what I want to tell you.

I'm going to try now, to share the words that often get trapped inside my own insecurity and worry.

I am grateful for you. I am thankful for you, and I love to be with you.

You make this world a safe place for me. Your companionship, love, and friendship allow me to feel more whole, and the love I feel for you is so clear and strong that sometimes it makes me want to break open. I know that sounds a bit much. But that is how I feel.

I am more myself with you than I can be on my own. I am more confident and gentle than I have ever been, and that transition is something I attribute to you.

You are my love, and I want you to know how very special you are to me.

These words are only a fraction of what I feel, but I hope they give you some notion of my love.

XO

Dear Love,

You have a romantic heart. It longs to be held and healed. It wants to do the work of loving.

This work, this work of love, is not easy. Love asks to be shared without protective layers. It asks to be trusted, to be known.

Approach love with authenticity, vulnerability, and bravery. I think you will find it is worth the effort.

Love yourself, you are worthy of it. Then, open that love to the world.

You have a beautiful gift to share. The recipient is a lucky soul.

XO

Dear Love,

Light found your shoulder in the almost dark, and from where I sat, propped up on the pillow, I could see clearly your beauty and power.

The rest of you was obscured by the darkest dark, but I know the rest of you well, and the rest of you was just as beautiful as what I could see, just there, touched by the morning light.

I did not want you to see me seeing.

I liked to watch you as if I were not there.

Your movements were true and full and unknowing of my eyes.

The light slid over you as you leaned down. My body warmed at this. The curve of your shoulder and the curve of your cheek held matching lines; both, to me, art.

Beautiful.

Beautiful.

Beautiful.

The light graced your breast, and then your hip, and then your thigh as you moved through the room in the almost dark.

The almost dark.

The almost dark.

Quietly, I watched as you slid into your clothes. The putting on felt to me as erotic as the taking off.

You moved through the room in a way that made me warm with want. I delighted in my body's tension, letting myself rise quietly as I watched.

Yes, I said, with everything but my lips.

Yes to the almost dark made bright, hot, and alive.

XO

Dear Love,

I look for you in the bookstore.

I look for you in the eyes of other patrons, and I look for you in the pages of the books. I know you are there somewhere.

I'm always looking.

There is something about the crisp pages, never turned, that creates excitement in me.

Sometimes I walk to the back of the bookstore, where the green emergency exit sign glows above the red door.

I turn and look through the tall aisles. Then I close my eyes, and I try to feel all the words and all the love in the words, and I pretend that we are in each book.

We are on a thousand adventures.

We learn physics, we learn the Kama Sutra, we go to war, we are parted and reunited. We are owls and foxes.

It's overwhelming to feel all of the words, but that overwhelm brings me closer to you.

That's how you feel to me, like millions of words and thousands of adventures.

I'm going to buy a book today. It will be you, and I will hold it and open it and smell it, and I will love it.

I'm not crazy. I don't think.

Today, I will find you in the bookstore again.

XO

Dear Love,

This morning, I watched the last leaf fall from the maple tree across the street. It glided to earth and tumbled across the road.

It is in the change of seasons that I most feel the change I made. Perhaps it is the empty trees that bring this to mind. This is a time when you can only see the sticks. The things at the center.

You are at the center of me. If I were to lose my things, if I were made bare, you would still be there. You are a limb. I could live without you. But I would not like it as much. That bit of truth can be seen in my choice to be here with you.

Now we can hold hands as much as we want to. I can share my day from across the room and not from across the country.

I know now that I would move around the world to be with you. That is something, isn't it? There is no other person I would choose. I choose you over my known place. I choose you over a new place with sun and palms. I choose you as my person to be close to.

I love you more than all the miles that used to be between us.

XO

Dear Love, I first saw you with your eyes on the night.
A million miles above, you were looking at starlight.
And dear god I lost my timing and my words felt all wrong.
So I wrote you a letter, then I wrote you a song.

Dear Love, I want to hold you, but all I've got is this pen.
So let me tell you everything: where do I begin?
You became the star of my life's show.
You became my dear love, I became your XO.

You wrote me back and told me that you felt the feeling too.
A letter every week, love, that's what I had to do.
Sipping coffee in the morning, holding hands in bed.
All these years together, all these letters read.
Pull out pen and paper and find words for us to sew.
You are the star of my life's show.

Dear Love, I want to hold you, but all I've got is this pen.
So let me tell you everything: where do I begin?
You became the star of my life's show.
You became my dear love, I became your XO.

You and me, love,
That's how the letter goes.
You my dear love,
Me your XO.

watch and listen: grantgosch.com

Grant Gosch is a writer and creative director based in the Pacific Northwest. He provides creative direction for global brands such as Nike and Intel while sharing his personal creative work through his books and storytelling performances.

Find him at @grantgosch